What Is the Most Important Invention?

by Mrs. Gaston's class
with Tony Stead

capstone®
classroom

Every day we use things that someone invented! Picture a regular school day. You wake up with the alarm clock, take a hot shower, and ride in a bus or a car to school. During the day you use computers and other devices and pay for things with money. But just think—alarm clocks, indoor plumbing, buses, cars, and computers are all inventions! Without inventions, our lives would be more difficult or, at least, boring! There are many inventions we use every day. But what's the most important invention? Some students in our class decided to choose the most important invention. Read this book to see if you are convinced!

The Electric Washing Machine

by Devon

In 1908, Alva J. Fisher invented something that made life a whole lot easier for many people—the electric washing machine! This invention is the most important one for several reasons.

First of all, the electric washing machine washes clothes much more quickly than people can wash them by hand. A job that used to take most of the day can now be done in about 30 minutes. This frees up the day for other important jobs or even for relaxing.

Here is a photograph of an electric washing machine used by people today.

In addition, people can also wash more clothes at a time. A washing machine can hold many more items than an old washtub. So laundry doesn't have to be done as often.

Finally, the washing machine makes housework less of a hassle. The machine does the work that used to be done by hand. While the machine is running, a person can do other things with his or her hands. This makes running the household much more efficient.

So when you put your clothes in the washer, think about what it would be like to have to wash clothes by hand. The washing machine is an incredibly important invention! It saves time, washes more clothes, and makes life easier if you want clean clothes.

People-Powered | Electric

Eyeglasses

by Zoe

Imagine that you were reading this book and the words looked a little blurry. You could probably put eyeglasses on to solve the problem! But people haven't always been able to use glasses. There are many different kinds of glasses and many different uses for them. People have been inventing and using optical aids since about AD 1000.

Why are glasses so important? You might have an optical disability like nearsightedness, farsightedness, or amblyopia (lazy eye). Without glasses, you could get a headache while reading—if you could read at all. You also need to see to do a lot of jobs. For instance, an adult with vision problems might not be able to safely drive a bus. Glasses aren't just convenient, they are necessary!

You might take glasses for granted if you wear them. But this invention is incredibly important. Without glasses, some readers couldn't read books, some athletes couldn't play their games, some drivers couldn't drive—the world would look very different to anyone with an eye problem.

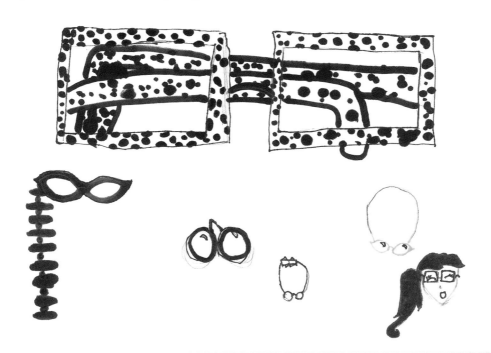

Bicycles

by Hawkins

Kirkpatrick Macmillan invented the first bicycle with pedals around 1839. The design and meaning of the bike has changed a lot over the years. But one thing has stayed the same—the bike is very important. To me, it's the most important invention.

Bikes are very convenient dollarwise. Instead of buying a car and having to pay a monthly car payment, you can buy a bike with just one payment and enjoy riding it. It also costs much less money to operate than a car or a motorcycle because a bike doesn't need gas.

Another reason that a bike is such an important invention is that you can get a lot of exercise from riding it. Why go to a fancy, expensive gym when you can ride a bike everywhere? It's a great use of energy and a good workout!

Last but not least, bicycles help you get through tight spaces that might be difficult to get through in a car.

The Smoke Detector

by Antonio

Buzz! Buzz! Buzz! An alarm wakes you up in the middle of the night. You are sleepy, but you smell smoke. A fire! It's a good thing the alarm woke you up—now you can head outside. The smoke detector is a very important invention. Francis Upton and Fernando Dibble invented the electric fire alarm in 1890. An updated form of their invention, the smoke detector, can be found in almost every home today.

The smoke detector warns people that a fire is nearby. When it detects smoke, it makes loud noises so people are warned and can get away from the danger.

This item saves lives. Because of the warning, people are able to get away from a fire when it starts.

The smoke detector saves money as well. When you know a fire has started, you can call the fire department right away or use a fire extinguisher to put out the flames. This saves the money needed for home repairs after a fire.

If you love your home and the people who live in it, the smoke detector is the most important invention. It warns people about fires and saves lives and money.

Electric Stove

by Jowan and Jarrett

Lloyd Groff Copeman made cooking easier for many people by inventing the electric stove. Before its invention in 1906, cooking was more difficult. The electric stove is a very important invention.

Electric stoves make cooking a lot easier because you can try many different recipes. Without a stove, a fire would have to be made. Cooking over a fire can be great, but there are some things you can't cook this way.

Electric stoves make cooking faster. It takes a long time for something to cook in a pot over a fire. You also don't have to build a fire and wait for it to be the right temperature to cook. You just turn the electric stove on, and minutes later, it's warm enough to cook your food.

Safety is important too, and the electric stove is a safe way to cook. A fire can burn you, but the stove is hot only in certain places. If you are careful, you won't get burned. Only your food will get warm!

In conclusion, the electric stove is the most important invention for people who love to cook and eat—so that's just about everyone! What do you think life would be like without this important invention?

FIRST Electric STOVE

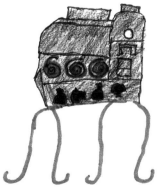

Today's ELECTRIC STOVE

The Flush Toilet

by Mary

Sir John Harrington built the first flush toilet for Queen Elizabeth in 1596. Now many people around the world use this important invention!

Before the invention of the flush toilet, conditions were very unsanitary. It was hard to get rid of waste and that caused diseases. Since good health is very important, this invention is one of the most important of all! The toilet is simple and easy to use. Flush toilets help keep the world clean and safe.

That's why I think they are the most important invention ever.

Woods

Chamber Pot

Chamber Pot Commode

First Flush Toilet

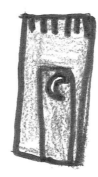

Outhouse

Now

Porta Potty

Microchips

by Ben

Many items that we use every day have microchips. Jack Kilby and Robert Noyce created this revolutionary and important invention in 1958 and 1959. Before the microchip, devices were huge! Now we can hold devices in our hands, making them easier to use and much more convenient to carry around.

Before the microchip, people saved data on paper. Now we save data on phones and computers. The amount of information we can store on one tiny data chip is huge! This makes it easy to store data and to find data that we need.

The microchip has made life better in many ways. Sure, we can use microchips to communicate. But microchips have also given us health benefits. Without microchips, for example, we would not have the bionic limbs that make life so much better for amputees.

The microchip is considered one of the most revolutionary pieces of technology ever. This invention has made electronics smaller, data-saving easier, and artificial limbs better. What would your life be like without the microchip?

Penicillin

by Jessi

Alexander Fleming discovered penicillin, an antibiotic, in 1928. Antibiotics are incredibly important because they treat people with infections that are caused by bacteria. Before the discovery of antibiotics, a simple infection could kill you. Can you imagine dying because of strep throat or an ear infection? Without penicillin, this could happen.

Many people around the world are safer, happier, and live longer lives because of penicillin. I can't imagine an invention more important than one that keeps people healthy.

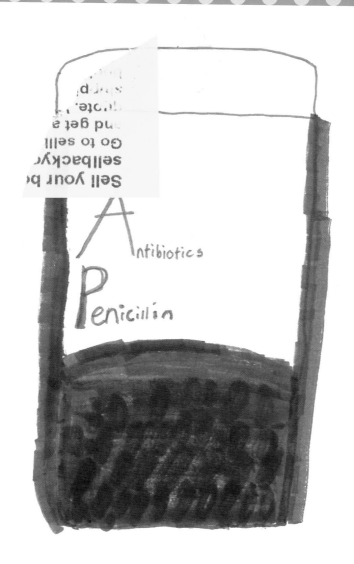

The Wheel

by Darsey

It's part of most methods of transportation. You can find it in gears and other important devices. What is it? It's the wheel! The wheel has always been one of the most important inventions of all time. Mesopotamians changed the world by being one of the first groups of people to use the wheel as early as 3500 BC. Today, wheels are all around us.

The wheel is a great invention because it helps things move easily. If you were to attach wheels to a small platform, you could move it without having to carry it. Long ago, this made it easier to move things from place to place, making trade possible!

Wheels help you move faster. Bicycles, cars, buses, trains, airplanes—all of these methods of transportation use wheels. Without wheels, we'd be stuck in one place.

Physics make wheels work. An object in motion tends to stay in motion. If you roll a wheel down a slight hill, that wheel stays in motion for a long time. Wheels make for less work.

I love the wheel! And, without the wheel, life would be very different—not nearly as good!

Our class thought of some interesting and important inventions! Our lives would be much different without these devices:

- electric washing machine
- eyeglasses
- bicycle
- smoke detector
- electric stove
- flush toilet
- microchip
- penicillin
- wheel

Which of these do you think is most important? Which argument was the most convincing?

Now, suppose you were writing the next pages of this book. Pick an invention. Why is it the most important invention? How could you prove it?